RETURN OF THE KILLER COAT

An entertaining follow-up to *Beware the Killer Coat*.

Susan Gates lives in County Durham. She has three children. She has written many children's books including *Sea Hags, Suckers and Cobra Sharks*; *Whizz Bang and the Crocodile Room* and the Walker titles *Beware the Killer Coat* (which won the Sheffield Children's Book Award) and *Don't Mess with Angels*. For older children her books include *Humanzee* and *Raider*, which was shortlisted for the Guardian Children's Fiction Award and Commended for the Carnegie Medal.

D0587684

Books by the same author

Beetle and the Biosphere
Beware the Killer Coat
Fisher Witch
Pet Swapping Day
Whizz Bang and the Crocodile Room

For older readers

Criss Cross
Don't Mess with Angels
Iron Heads
Raider

SUSAN GATES

RETURN of the KILLER COAT

Illustrations by Josip Lizatović

For Annie

659057
MORAY COUNCIL
Department of Technical
& Leisure Services
JB

First published 1998 by
Walker Books Ltd, 87 Vauxhall Walk
London SE11 5HJ

This edition published 1999

2 4 6 8 10 9 7 5 3 1

Text © 1998 Susan Gates
Illustrations © 1998 Josip Lizatović

This book has been typeset in Garamond.

Printed in England

British Library Cataloguing in Publication Data
A catalogue record for this book is
available from the British Library.

ISBN 0-7445-6391-7

CONTENTS

CHAPTER 1

"Hi, Andrew," said someone. "What do you think of my new coat?"

I turned round. It was the day of our trip to the forest. Our class was waiting for the coach. My best friend Alice had just joined the crowd.

And guess what? I couldn't believe my eyes!

She was wearing my old enemy, the Killer Coat.

I was really shocked. "Not you again," I muttered in a grim voice. "I thought we'd got rid of you."

I went rushing up to Alice.

Not you again!

"Look, it's a really good coat, isn't
it?" she said, twirling round proudly.
"I got it at a jumble sale."

"No, it isn't a really good coat!"
I shouted at her. "It's a really bad
coat, actually!"

When I had the
Killer Coat, it was
big and bad and
dangerous. It was
red then – with a
red tongue and
mean green eyes
and sharp silver teeth.

It doesn't look dangerous now.
Not since it shrank in our
washing machine. It
looks cute and pink
now. But don't let
that fool you.
It's still the same
old Killer Coat
underneath.

"Don't wear that coat, Alice!"
I begged her. "Don't put anything in
its pockets! It ate my gloves. It ate
poor Ratty, my pet rat. Then it tried
to eat *me*. It's a wicked, wicked coat!"

"Go away, Andrew," said Alice. "You're in one of your silly moods."

Alice put the hood up and suddenly vanished inside the coat!

The coat's little pink eyes glowed like hot coals. I knew what that meant! Oh no, I thought. It's up to its old tricks. It's trying to eat her already!

I peered into the hood. All
I could see was a black hole, with
Alice's eyes sparkling right at the
bottom.

And the Killer Coat had a big, fat
smile on its face. Like a python
that's just swallowed its dinner.

I leapt at the coat and grabbed it. "You horrible coat!" I yelled. "Don't you dare eat my friends!"

I wrestled with the coat. I shook its sleeves. I tugged the hood: "Let – Alice – go!"

"Andrew!" shouted our teacher. "What on earth are you doing? Leave Alice alone. Stop hurting her!"

"I'm not hurting her! I'm saving her from the Killer Coat!"

Then POP! the hood came off. Alice was free!

Phew! I thought. It's let her go. It's let her go, this time.

But I was in disgrace. Our teacher said, "Andrew, I didn't know you were a bully."

"I'm *not* a bully, I'm not!" I said.

But it was no use. She thought *I* was the villain! She made me sit on my own in the coach. So I couldn't warn Alice. Even though I knew that she was in deadly danger.

CHAPTER 2

In the forest Alice said, "I'm going to climb that tree."

I said, "I'll come with you."

But Alice said, "No thank you, Andrew. I don't like bullies."

"I'm *not* a bully!" I tried to explain, but she wouldn't listen.

Alice and the Killer Coat went climbing together. I was left behind. I felt really lonely and sad.

Behind Alice's back, the coat stuck out its pink floppy tongue as if to say, "Na, na, na, na, Andrew! I'm Alice's best friend now! Nobody likes you any more!"

HELP! HELP!

Suddenly, KERRACK! I heard a branch snapping.

"Help, help!" cried Alice. "I'm falling!"

I ran like the wind. "I'll save you Alice!" I cried.

But the Killer Coat
saved her first. It
spiked its sleeve
on the broken
branch so Alice
couldn't fall.
Then it
stretched its
arm like a
bungee rope
and lowered
Alice safely to
the ground.

"Your coat saved you from falling!" said our teacher. "You could have had a nasty accident."

"Did you hear what Miss Miller said?" Alice told everyone. "She said my coat saved me! My coat is the bravest, most wonderful coat in the whole wide world!"

The coat puffed itself up like a big pink marshmallow. It looked really pleased with itself.

And Alice thought it was a big, big hero.

I lay under a tree and closed my eyes. I imagined I was the big hero. I was bold Sir Andrew, a knight on a white horse.

Sir Killer Coat was on a black horse. We were jousting. Everyone in my class was watching. And I was everyone's favourite.

Sir Andrew!

"Boo!" they hissed at the evil Sir Killer Coat. "Hurray, bold Sir Andrew!" they cried.

I was winning the fight. Sir Killer Coat tumbled off its horse. I was the jousting champion!

Everyone cheered like mad. "Sir Andrew! Sir Andrew! Our hero!"

I opened my eyes. Nothing had changed. Alice was still being kind to the Killer Coat.

"You poor coat," she was saying. "You've got a nasty tear in your sleeve. I'll have to stick a plaster on that."

I thought, I've got to get rid of that coat. I've got to get rid of it once and for all!

CHAPTER 3

I was just thinking, But *how* can
I get rid of it? when Miss Miller said,
"Time for our picnic."

Alice searched in the pockets of
the Killer Coat. "I'm sure I had an
apple in here," she said. "A big, red
apple."

Miss Miller said, "Oh dear, it must
have fallen out."

"No!" I cried. "It didn't fall out!
The coat ate it! I told you it ate
things! I told you it was dangerous!"

They didn't believe me. They
looked at me as if I was crazy.

But I knew I was right. Because
the coat gave me a wolfish grin with
its sharp little teeth
as if to say,
"Yum, yum,
that was a
nice crunchy
apple. Now
what am
I going to
crunch up
next?"

Miss Miller said, "Who wants to play softball?"

Alice said, "I do!"

She took off the coat because it was too hot to run in. She left it on the picnic table.

Soon everyone was running to play softball. But I stayed behind. I was busy scooping out a big, big hole underneath a tree.

When the hole was deep enough I said, "In you go!" to the Killer Coat. But it wouldn't go in. It was fighting back! *Whop*, an arm shot out and slapped my ear! I crammed it back into the hole.

WHOP!

"Get in, you villain!" I panted.

"Grrrr!" I heard it snarl.

It came bulging out of the hole like pink lava from a volcano.

Those silver teeth were sharp as spikes. I wasn't going to put my fingers near those.

So I poked it back in with a stick.

"You … stay … in … there!" I told it.

I filled in the hole with dirt.

I stamped it flat.

"Let's see you get out of that!"

I said, rubbing my hands.

Alice came back from playing softball. "Where's my coat?" she said. "My coat that saved me from falling. Have you seen it, Andrew?"

"No," I shrugged, looking innocent.

Then Miss said, "Shhh, children, can you see what I see?"

It was a baby squirrel. It came bouncing across the grass. Then it stopped, underneath the tree – and started digging for nuts, like squirrels do.

Oh no! I thought. Don't dig there, little squirrel!

Too late! An angry pink eye was glaring up out of the ground. The eye swivelled around. It spotted the baby squirrel. It started to glow.

I yelled, "Watch out, squirrel!" I jumped up and down. I waved my arms about like mad!

The squirrel scampered away. Phew! I thought. That was close!

Miss Miller said, "Andrew, you naughty boy! You scared that poor little squirrel…"

I started to say, "I wasn't scaring it, I was *saving* it…" when Alice cried out, "There's my coat!"

She pulled the coat out of the ground. She shook the dirt off it.

"Poor coat!" she said. "All alone in that deep, dark hole. How did you get in there?"

Everyone crowded round.
Everyone made a big fuss. As if it
was the most famous coat in the
world!

Behind their backs, the Killer Coat gave me a wicked grin as if to say, "See Andrew, you can't get rid of *me* that easily! I am *indestructible!*"

CHAPTER 4

That night I had a dream about the Killer Coat. I dreamed it was the most famous coat in the world. It had its picture in all the papers.

HERO COAT SAVES ALICE FROM FALLING! the headlines said.

The coat was
interviewed on
television. It smiled
and smiled at the
cameras with its sparkly silver teeth.
"You must be really brave," said
the lady interviewer.

And the Killer Coat shrugged and looked modest, as if to say, "It was nothing. Any coat would have done the same."

The Killer Coat rode about in a big car. It had sunglasses on. It waved at the crowds through the window.

It signed autographs for its fans. They all cheered and cheered. "We love you, Hero Coat!" they cried.

I dreamed that the coat went to Buckingham Palace in a top hat. It got a medal for bravery from the Queen.

It was even a guest on National
Lottery Live. Everyone loved it.

Only I said, "Don't trust it. It's a Killer Coat, really. It ate Ratty, my pet rat. It nearly ate a baby squirrel! It'll eat *you*, if you don't watch out!"

But nobody took any notice of me. I was only a little kid. My warnings were drowned by the cheers of the crowd.

CHAPTER 5

Next day I walked into the school playground. There was Alice wearing the Killer Coat.

Its silver teeth seemed as sharp as scissors. Its pink, piggy eyes were hot and fierce.

Only I saw how
dangerous it was.

I even thought
I heard it growl:
"Grrrr!" It was trying
to scare me away.
It wanted Alice all
to itself.

"What are you
doing, Alice?"

"I'm climbing this
tree."

"But we're not
allowed to do that.
What if you fall?"

"I won't fall," said
Alice.

Maybe she thought the Killer Coat would save her, just like it did in the forest!

"No, don't trust it. It's evil. It's only pretending to be good," I cried.

"What on earth are you talking about Andrew?" said Alice halfway up the trunk.

I could hardly bear to look. I had to peep through my fingers.

47

Then, suddenly, Alice's feet
slipped off a slippery branch!

"I'm falling!" she cried.

The Killer Coat stopped
pretending. It changed to a monster
in mid-air! It opened its jaws. It
roared like Tyrannosaurus Rex.

ROARRRRRR!

"Alice!" I cried, rushing to save her.
I held out my arms to catch her.
I missed. But she had a safe landing
after all because *whump!* she landed
in the sandpit.

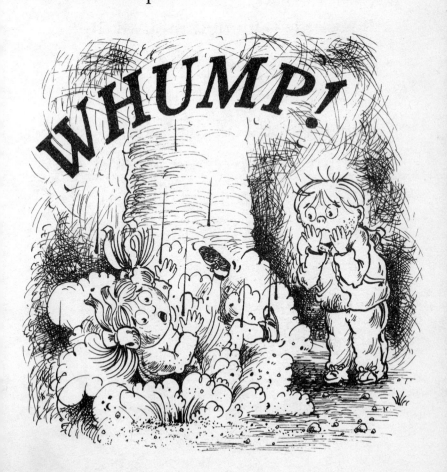

She staggered to her feet. "Are you all right, Alice?" I asked anxiously.

She wasn't hurt. But she was in a really bad mood.

"Stupid coat!" she said. "It's all crumpled now! It's full of sand! I can't wear it like that!"

Alice ripped off the Killer Coat. She hurled it on to the ground. It lay in the grass like a big pink puddle with its tongue hanging out.

"I've really gone off that coat," Alice said, as she marched away into school.

CHAPTER 6

But it's not so easy to get rid of the
Killer Coat. Miss Miller came into
our classroom. She said, "Alice, you
left your coat on the grass. So I
rescued it and hung it on a peg in
the cloakroom."

Aargh! I thought. The Killer Coat always comes back!

Then I heard Alice whisper, "Bother! I don't want that old coat any more. I want a nice new one."

So I whispered, "Don't worry, Alice. I'll help you get a new coat."

We made an excuse to leave the class. We rushed straight to the cloakroom.

This time, I thought, I'm going to get rid of that Killer Coat *for good*.

There was the Killer Coat. It was hanging around with the other coats, trying to look innocent.

But, of course, I wasn't fooled.

My brain was full of crazy ideas.

Blast it in a rocket to Mars. Chuck it in a volcano. Then suddenly I spotted something.

The plaster Alice had stuck on the Killer Coat was hanging off. I could see the tear underneath. The tear had a long thread dangling from it. "What do you think would happen," I asked Alice, "if I just pulled this dangly bit of cotton?" As I went near, the coat seemed to puff itself up. It hissed at me, "*SSSSS!*" like a cobra.

I snatched my hand back. Then
I thought, Be brave! So I grabbed
that thread and gave it a tug.

It came wriggling out like a worm.
It got longer and longer, like a magic
trick, as if it would never stop!

Then guess what? A sleeve fell off the Killer Coat! *Flop*! right on to the floor. I pulled more thread. More stitches came out. *Flop*! the other sleeve fell off.

The coat was coming to bits, right before our eyes. I kept on pulling. *Plop*! the hood fell off.

"Ha ha! You can't hurt anyone now," I said. "Not now you're all in pieces!"

And Alice said, "My mum will have to buy me a new coat now! Thanks, Andrew!"

We picked up the bits of the
Killer Coat and took them outside
and stuffed them into the bin.
We slammed down the lid and put
a rock on it. Just to make sure.

"Hurray!" we shouted.

I couldn't believe it. It was all over. I felt like the bold Sir Andrew! I had overcome the fiercest foe.

Now pet rats will be safe. Baby squirrels will be safe. And *you* will be safe from the terrible Killer Coat.

YAY!

"Yay!" I cheered.
"I am the champion.
The Killer Coat is DEAD!"

MORE WALKER SPRINTERS

For You to Enjoy

☐ 0-7445-3666-9   *Beware the Killer Coat*
by Susan Gates/Josip Lizatović   £3.50

☐ 0-7445-5499-3   *Free the Whales*
by Jamie Rix/Mike Gordon   £3.50

☐ 0-7445-3188-8   *Beware Olga!*
by Gillian Cross/Arthur Robins   £3.50

☐ 0-7445-6011-X   *Auntie Billie's Greatest Invention*
by Judy Allen/Chris Mould   £3.50

☐ 0-7445-6044-6   *Emmelina and the Monster*
by June Crebbin/Tony Ross   £3.50

☐ 0-7445-6017-9   *The Polecat Café*
by Sam Llewellyn/Arthur Robins   £3.50

☐ 0-7445-5407-1   *Elena the Frog*
by Dyan Sheldon/Sue Heap   £3.50

**Walker Paperbacks are available from most booksellers,
or by post from B.B.C.S., P.O. Box 941, Hull, North Humberside HU1 3YQ**

24 hour telephone credit card line 01482 224626

To order, send: Title, author, ISBN number and price for each book ordered, your full
name and address, cheque or postal order payable to BBCS for the total amount and allow
the following for postage and packing: UK and BFPO: £1.00 for the first book, and 50p
for each additional book to a maximum of £3.50. Overseas and Eire: £2.00 for the first
book, £1.00 for the second and 50p for each additional book.

Prices and availability are subject to change without notice.

Name _____

Address _____

_____